Norwalk, OH
A Novel

By Michael Hanck

Copyright © 2015 Michael Hanck

All rights reserved.

ISBN: 151439796X
ISBN-13: 978-1514397961

DEDICATION

For Northern Ohio; Be Well.

And for Pam Mellen, Elizabeth Poggiali, and Leslie Sapp-Petrie for teaching me about the English language, grammar, vocabulary and stuff.

TABLE OF "CONTENTS"

	Disclaimer	i
1	Section 1	3
2	Section 2	7
3	Section 3	14
4	Section 4	18
5	Section 5	23
6	Section 6	27
7	Section 7	33
8	Section 8	48
9	Section 9	57
10	Section 10	69
11	Section 11	73
12	Section 12	84
14	Section 14	88
15	Section 15	93
16	Section 16	110
17	Section 17	116
18	Section 18	130
19	Section 19	143
20	Section 20	150
21	Section 21	163
22	Section 22	166
23	Section 23	173
24	Section 24	184

DISCLAIMER

Norwalk, OH by Michael Hanck is a work of fiction. All of the characters and events in this novel have been created by the author. Any likenesses to actual people and/or events are purely coincidental. The views, opinions, and values of the various characters, including the narrator, do not necessarily represent either the views, opinions, or values of Michael Hanck, his family, friends, associates, or acquaintances. This is a work of literary fiction, and it is not intended to portray actual people and/or events.

THE BEGINNING

Usually, when in search of someone, one will begin with some sort of a lead…

Searching for someone is like the art of composing a biography. You want to find out as much as you can about the person, making sure, all the while, that the information is reliable, recordable, and somehow illuminating – or inspiring.

One can go to that person's hometown. One could try to track down that person's family, friends, and acquaintances, perform interviews, and learn something new and novel about him or her. There might be letters or papers, like unintentional clues, that he or she has left for others to discover; they can be as tedious as travel receipts or hastily-jotted notes. More helpful are the works that other people have composed about that person, biographies or reviews of that person's work, which make the person's paper trail more obvious while still leaving room for further inquiry.

When, however, that someone who you are searching for is your self, the task becomes much more difficult. You are already in or have been through your hometown, wherever that might be.

But who do you interview to learn about your self? Who can give an adequate analysis of your self, a holistic appraisal? What papers or letters of yours do you read? Who are you to have a biography or review of your work? Even then, do you trust those assessments of your self? More so, do you trust your own assessments? Finally, can you believe your own writings and notes, self-justifying as they probably, and rightly, appear? Where do you go? Where do you start?

I have never been much of a wise person, but this much, about the difficulty of learning about your self, has occurred to me, or, rather, has been given to me.

To be honest, for most of my life, I have been a dealer in small lies. In the art of trying to become something, to become someone, I have, like so many of the people I've known, told my self little lies about my self to my self until they became true, until I, and others, started believing them. It is the creation of credentials, the stating of intention, and the hopeful making of plans, all on the shifty ground of becoming a person in the world. This is how a new person is often born into the world.

Regardless of how that act of creation turns out, there is always, for every person, a starting place, a point of departure, yes, I'm talking about a lead.

For me, that was Norwalk, OH.

IN NORWALK, OHIO

When I graduated from college in my early twenties, full of ideas, loaded with debt, and sorely lacking in wisdom, I found myself back at home. So far in life, my aims had been rather small: graduate, graduate again, and then – well – what?

After graduation, I moved back to my hometown, Norwalk, Ohio, which was a place once fabulous, with a nice downtown and "nice" church-going folk, but was now a place that was soaked in drugs (especially cocaine and heroin) and alcohol, rundown, and as economically promising as the rest of the post-industrial rust belt.

Even Charles Dickens, the British author, champion of the poor becoming rich, of the underdog succeeding, slammed Norwalk, Ohio. In his book, *American Notes*, Dickens described Norwalk as stale, boring, something like the back of an English watering hole out of season. Even he, back then, saw the destiny of Norwalk, Ohio and the little cities around it, a destiny of obscurity, of being out of season, of falling into nothingness.

While at home, I aimed to complete another small goal in life, to substitute teach in my old school district, to see those old buildings and classrooms once again, to figure out what it had all meant, to look back from a distance, to be more objective, and to come to some conclusions about the earliest part of my life.

Instead of finding a fantastic world,

warm nostalgia, and some wisdom through later more-objective reflection, I found myself waking up to phone calls at 5:00 a.m., rushing to get ready, arriving at a strange building, not knowing anyone anymore, studying a lesson plan hurriedly in hopes of somehow fulfilling it (if there even was a lesson plan to be spoken of), and pushing knowledge onto students who knew that I was only but a temporary authority figure. To say, at all, that I was an authority figure is just another little necessary lie. In truth, I was still a scared kid, trying to figure out what was going on, what I was supposed to be doing with my life.

In this sort of situation, after weeks of either waking up to a phone call that would send me rushing out of the door or waking up to nothing at all but disappointment and a day of financial fretting, it did not take me long to come to the conclusion that I was in trouble. The idea, whether real or just imagined, that I had failed thus far in life crept up on me slowly, like an army of mayflies scaling up the side of a house, smothering it. This feeling started off small, like my own little lies, with those financial worries, with all that fretting about making money, and the feeling itself soon turned into whole days, days wasted away in a breakfast diner, wondering what more I could be doing with my life, brooding over a cup of lukewarm decaf coffee, my shirt unbuttoned at the top, my tie loose and drooping hopelessly down, crooked and useless. Perhaps this was the truth.

The situation would not have been so

bad had I lived, thus far, another life. I imagined myself having grown up in another place, another region. I imagined being born in Connecticut, having cities full of affluent people around me, a better economy, an arts scene, one with theatre and dramatic readings and paintings and local artists and book groups and author meet-and-greets, having access, when the time came, to big-name colleges, to ivy league battleships, and from these places, launching out into a life where I could happily skip over the rust belt, not knowing or needing to know much about its existence, having dinners in New York City, with important people, having money to drop on such a dinner, being flashy and picking up the entire check with a wave and a cheeky laugh. Or, perhaps, growing up in the Pacific Northwest, maybe Seattle. Growing up there, I would, inevitably, pick up some talent or skill (from merely living in the region!), such as a phenomenal musical ability, in addition, of course, to other helpful and popular hobbies, such as long-boarding or surf-boarding or something-boarding. I would be more environmentally conscious, and thus better prepared for the future, maybe getting a job in the sustainable energy industry. I would know great bands before they became popular, I would understand trends before they spread, and I would have a foothold in a temperate and much-desired region of the nation, where young people flock instinctively like migrating birds. All of this would allow me to better network, to be, for lack of a better word, cool. I would be cool. I would be successful. I would be a Charles

Dickens character, pulling myself up from the bottom to a well-lived, well-ordered life. I would make it.

Instead, I had, thus far, lived my life as I had always lived it. I was in Norwalk, Ohio, in a place where, for the first eighteen years of my life, all I did was burn bridges.

OF AN UNBECOMING PERSON

Having grown up in such a place, having always sensed somehow that I wanted more than it had to offer me, I had, as a kid, reacted in ways that I lived to regret. At the time, they had made enough sense to me. At the time, they had given me something to do, perhaps a little humor to take the edge off of my discontentment.

In retrospect, well…

I had, for a shortlist of my sins, toilet-papered my band director's house a total of a dozen times, in just one month, which was December, argued incredibly and insultingly with anyone in town who happened to disagree with me about nearly anything, pressured my friends into pranking other people to the point of extreme irritation and agitation, then, in turncoat fashion, pranked my own friends, dabbled in other illegal things that we need not talk about anymore, and, to sum it all up rather nicely, had been a real jerk in general.

I still don't want to talk about it, to be honest.

Yet, for all of this, I never actually harmed anyone physically or cost anyone a great deal of money. We never destroyed property. We did, underneath it all, care enough to not cost anyone anything substantial. I was just really good at being a jerk. But, as seems to be the truth of the matter, people do not care enough to differentiate between the two. Being an irritant, whether harmful or not, makes one into a person better avoided, which is the same outcome that the harmful person receives - minus potential jail time. One need not break any formal laws to be a criminal. This is especially the case in a small town, in the rust belt, in Norwalk, Ohio.

So, during those days, alone at the breakfast diner in Norwalk, Ohio, over a cup of lukewarm coffee, which was undoubtedly made with the blandest of Arabica beans, I had plenty of time to think of who I had been, of why I was in the rust belt, of how my life could have been different, and about the nowhere to which my life was heading - and quick.

A line from church popped into my head - the quick and the dead. I never knew before that they could be the same thing. I had never really known that.

BY SOME GRACE

By some grace, I still, somehow, had retained those friends whom I had pressured into pranking other people: classmates, elders, mentors, and authority figures.

My only saving grace seemed to be the now threadbare connections I had made with those four friends: John, Jeffrey, Cory, and Keith.

Unfortunately, however, they too had burned bridges, some more than others.

John, the youngest son of a single mother, was a good enough person, but like me (almost too much like me) he was prone to argue with people and insult them. Our friendship worked best when that person who was being argued with or who was being insulted was not the other one of us. Unfortunately, this was not often the case between us. Yet, I should add that, underneath these similarities, there was an incredibly sensitive person in John; it could be hard to see under the numerous layers of misplaced humor and the hint of strong leadership potential left untapped, but it was there.

Jeffrey, who had become, often, the victim of our pranks and hijinks, didn't, for whatever reason, want to reveal too much of himself to us. He was always a very private person, and this caused us to push him, to provoke him, all the more. He couldn't have shared any less with us. Many years later, he would get married, right in Norwalk, without letting any of us know in advance, we being his closest friends.

Cory, very soon after high school, had developed a powerful cocaine addiction. It started off harmlessly enough. It was, at first, a sidebar to his daily activities, but eventually, perhaps because of the wretched feeling that accompanies one's coming down off of that spectacular high, of the cocaine wearing off and reality dripping back into one's brain, he dove into the substance much more heavily. While all of us, to some degree, had rebelled and rejected the faded advice of others, especially our elders and mentors, we regarded Cory's deepening addiction with a sort of silent horror, afraid that, by confronting it, we would destroy the very threads that knit us into a brotherhood. What we didn't realize, until it was too late, was that the threads were fraying as quickly as dopamine could hit the brain. By the time that confrontation was absolutely necessary, we had been robbed and tricked and disappointed enough to let him go his own way, to smile and nod in his direction but to do so with our eyes off of his and, instead, latched onto the door, waiting, desperately, to escape.

This left, at that time, my friendship with Keith. The other friendships, even though still valued in remembrance and memorial, had unraveled enough for them to feel lacking. I was running out of connections.

Keith, unlike the others at that point, had also finished college, which made neither him nor I better than the others but which did serve to give us something more in common and thus more of a chance to revive and redefine our friendship. He also, by some good fortune, shared my unfettered desire for fun, novelty, and adventure, as sheltered from that as we had been in growing up in the rust belt.

Our dreams of greatness and our hunger for thrill reached up high, hoping to be noticed by some giant pair of human eyes floating in the sky. We were, to say the least, callous in our hope that our lives actually meant something.

THE ART OF BECOMING

It was December, on yet another day without work, when Keith called. He was not often in town in those days, being a graduate student at The Ohio State University and who, through the program there, would soon be living in Xalapa while finishing up his Master's Degree in Education. Since it was Winter Vacation, Keith was back to visit for a short time. Soon, however, he would be back in Nothern Ohio for good, having obtained his Master's Degree, and, as we had hoped he would receive, working a job in a nice, nearby school system, as oxymoronic as I thought that to be.

I was, as to be expected, at the diner, having decaf coffee and wondering about all manner of things by myself, when he called.

"Hello?"

"Peter! Peter, how are you?"

"Hey Keith, I thought you were going to be too busy to hang out this time around…"

"No, no, not too busy at all. Hey, we're getting a group together tonight, just to hang out, have a few drinks, talk about old times. Do you want to come?"

Having nothing better to do, I was able to make up my mind rather quickly.

"Yeah, sure. What time? Where?"

"I'll come by and pick you up. Let's

say...about 7ish?"

"7? Yeah, sure. 7 it is then."

"Ok, well, I got to go, busy running errands with my mom - you know how it is - but I'll see you around 7, ok?"

He was always running errands with his mom. Why was he always running errands with his mom?

"Looking forward to it."

"Ok, buh-bye now."

"Bye."

I hung up, finished my coffee, and pushed aside my plate with the half-eaten short stack of soggy pancakes. I left twenty dollars, enough for the bill and the tip, and walked out of the breakfast diner. I spent the rest of that morning, and the early afternoon, wandering around Norwalk, looking at the historic buildings downtown, trying to imagine what they had once been in their days of glory and what they could now be instead, doing my best to avoid going home, to avoid showing everyone there that, once again, I had failed to land a job.

IN A MOMENT

Later that evening, after finally finishing *The Picture of Dorian Gray*, I went out to the porch to have a smoke and wait for Keith to show up. I had been, in my spare time during the last of couple weeks, returning to the works of literary giants such as Wilde and Steinbeck and Fitzgerald, working my way through their masterpieces, paying attention to the tempo and the tone, the general warp and woof of their texts. They provided a nice break from reality, a rest stop of sorts. It passed the time in a rewarding way.

I had intended to start reading non-fiction books, but I hadn't started yet. I had one book, *Tell Them Who I*

Am, which was about women who were homeless. I was half-eager to read it, but I couldn't get myself to do it. In college, I had read through Dorothy Day's *The Long Lonliness* and had fallen in love with social justice, but being back in Norwalk, those college days felt far away. I had really enjoyed learning about serving people in poverty at that time, but more and more, I was coming to recognize that time period as a passing college phase, like all of those people in the last generation who "really got into" Liberation Theology while they were in school.

I glanced at my watch. It was almost 7:30 p.m. and I had not heard from Keith since that morning. I wasn't sure if he'd still show up. I smoked two cigarettes, right in a row, and was thinking about the character Lord

Wotton, when, just shortly after 7:45 p.m., Keith's dark red HHR pulled up in my driveway. I filed away my thoughts for a later time, made my way down the steps, and walked toward the HHR. I realized that two other people were in the car with Keith. I hadn't expected that. At first, I was a little confused, looking at the car again as though I wasn't sure it was the right one. Sure enough though, Keith's big grinning face was behind the wheel, all smiles. With his right hand, in one quick sure gesture, he beckoned me to just get into the damn car already.

Keith, unlike the rest of us, had not burned many bridges. He was included in our little group, but oftentimes, he was the victim of our mischief rather than a co-perpetrator of it.

The best example of this is a time when he was at his home alone. His parents had gone out of town for some sort of event, perhaps a wedding or something, and he was by himself, in his room, with a single light on, studying. John, Cory, and I had crept up on his house, which was on a main street not far from downtown Norwalk. Cory had a long line of firecrackers. His job was to light this chain of firecrackers, throw it onto the jagged stone steps leading up to the house's side door, and run away with John and I, all the way around the corner to John's car, and escape. Cory lit the fuse and threw the chain of firecrackers, but instead of tossing them onto the stone steps, he threw them onto Keith's wooden porch, up against the front door. All at the same time, we started running and yelling, "Oh shit!" The chain of firecrackers went off, leaving little burn marks all over the porch, with not just a few exploding on his beautiful green front door. There was loud cracking, a bursting apart of the peaceful silence that night, a shadow in the window falling to the ground, and three skinny teenagers running through the anonymity of the night and around the corner, trying to just get away. It turns out that, after picking himself up off of the floor, Keith called the Fire Department, who then showed up and had to file a report. In school the next day, Keith and some of the school officials began asking us questions. None of us knew anything; we had all been at home, studying, which was, in part, true. It was a month before Keith talked to or trusted any of us again. Then - it was a full year before we told Keith the truth about what had happened, because, by that time, no one, neither him nor the authorities, cared anymore.

(So I guess we did accidentally damage just a little property...)

Thus, it should not have surprised me to see Keith with a nearly full car. He hadn't done the things that the rest of us had done. He was of a different sort...

To be honest, I wasn't even sure what we were going to be doing that night. I had simply agreed to whatever it was. I only hoped that it wouldn't be boring. And so, being agreeable, being friendly, I just got into the damn car.

IT JUST HAPPENS

To my surprise, it was neither John nor Cory in the car. It wasn't even Jeffrey. Instead, it was two girls, only one of whom I knew.

In the passenger's seat sat this beautiful blonde girl, Ursula. Keith introduced us.

"Peter, this is Ursula. She's from Germany. She's still learning English, so please just understand."

I thought that was a rather ironic thing for him to say, but I decided not to voice it.

We shook hands and she smiled, her perfect teeth almost blinding me in the process.

"Nice to meet you," I said.

"It is good to meet you too, Peter," she said with a heavy German accent.

Perhaps she was better at this than I assumed.

As for the other person, I knew her from high school, though we had never been close and had rarely ever talked. Undoubtedly though, she knew of me, had heard about me. Her name was Katie Austin. She was the daughter of a wealthier couple, living as they did in a gated community on the lake. Her dad was some sort of engineer. He obviously made good money. Her mother was a well-respected teacher in one of the Norwalk elementary schools. They held membership at the local Methodist Church, where all of the wealthy people went, and were, actually, very good people, *nice* people. Katie was, currently, obtaining her Master's Degree in Occupational Therapy, looking to help people, aiming to make decent money, and hoping to become, I assumed, a member in good standing of whichever community she ended up in. I would learn all of this later that same night. For the time being, however, I only knew that she was a) upper class and b) very nice. I joined her in the backseat.

Keith backed the HHR out of my driveway, and began, as is typical of him, a long monologue. I settled into my seat, wondering what business I had being in this car with these people. What was I really doing here?

"Peter, I'm so glad that you could come with us to celebrate Katie's birthday. It can be so hard to get people to come out sometimes and so many people are gone, but you know how it is."

I wished he had let me know the occasion sooner.

"So, we're going downtown to celebrate. And, sorry I didn't tell you about Ursula sooner. I wanted to surprise you. So, and Katie already knows this, Ursula is visiting with me from OSU; we're going to Mexico together."

The English-speaking German was going to Mexico.

"We met at school. Ursula is studying Spanish, and Education too, and well, we will be, while in Mexico, taking classes at the University of Xalapa. And we decided it might be nice for her to come visit Northern Ohio."

I wondered why.

"So she's getting to see what things are like here and meet my folks and whatnot, but anyway, how rude of me, how are you, Peter?"

I didn't know what to tell them.

"I'm doing fine. Substitute teaching, seeing people, saving up money. You know how it is."

"I do, I do," Keith replied, "Everything is so expensive nowadays! But, hey! Tonight, we're going to have fun, not worry about that, right, Katie?"

She released a quick, almost-silent chuckle, directed to herself more than anybody else, and then agreed with him.

"Yes," she said, and then, touching me lightly on the shoulder, she added, "So, Peter, Keith tells me that you're thinking of going to Mexico too."

This was news to me, but for whatever reason, perhaps simply to avoid an awkward situation where Keith was exposed, I replied, "Yeah, we've been talking about that a lot lately."

Keith quickly jumped in, knowing that he had some explaining to do later.

"Yes, Peter's seriously considering going, and so I've been telling him all about Mexico, about how much fun we'll have down there, about how nice it will be to get away." Then, briefly looking over his right shoulder at me, he said, "Peter, you'll love it. It's not that expensive, and you'll be staying with me anyway. And there's so much to do! And we'll do quite a bit of traveling too. It'll be a good time, nice and relaxing. You need it with how much you've been working lately."

"Yeah, I'm sure I do."

By the time we arrived downtown, Keith had, apparently, talked me into going to Mexico, albeit covertly. Though, to be honest, I wasn't sure if that was, in reality, the case.

Was this how our friendship worked?

We passed over some of the sketchier bars, the ones to which I was most accustomed, and found a nicer one. We showed our IDs to the bouncer, went in, and grabbed four seats at the corner of the bar, two of us on each side. Ursula and Keith, of course, sat together on one side, with Keith nearer the end, and Katie and I sat on the other side, with my being further from the edge of the bar. Keith, as could be depended upon, ran the conversation, keeping things going, making himself laugh and thus making the rest of us laugh as well. Perhaps it was all the talk about Mexico, about all of the money that I would need, money that I didn't have - or perhaps I was just thirsty, but during my third or fourth glass of scotch, I suddenly realized how much I had been drinking.

I was actually having a pretty good time. Soon thereafter, I was in the thick fray of the conversation, telling stories from the good old days when we would run amok, when we didn't care, making jokes, laughing at things, whatever they were, and I had the feeling as though this moment was all that mattered. Life, at the moment, was complete cacophony.

It seemed like everyone else was having a pretty good time as well. Keith, being our driver, was taking it easy now, letting us run more of the conversation and drinking quite a bit less. Katie had, since our arrival, really loosened up; she too was making jokes now. Since it was her birthday, the rest of us were taking good care of her, buying round after round of shot after shot, and it wasn't long before she was hugging us and smiling at everything.

At some point, a man in raggedy clothes appeared. He was wearing blue jeans with a hole in the right knee and one, still in formation, on his rear. His shirt had a big picture of a lion on the front, from some animated movie I guessed. For some reason, I found this to be hysterical and had to excuse myself to go and finish laughing on the far side of the room. The man didn't speak very clearly, but he was friendly enough; he was probably intoxicated. But - he was a good sport. Eventually, gaining some composure, I was able to make my way back to the bar and take a seat, though, I will admit, it was hard to hold my composure.

Katie told him that it was her birthday, for what reason I don't know, but he responded by buying her another drink. Keith was, subtly, covertly, making fun of the man, but the man didn't seem to notice as he just laughed along with the rest of us. He had a few more drinks himself and afterwards decided to propose to Katie, giving her a ring off of his finger. She found this to be incredibly humorous, putting the ring on and posing for pictures with it. Oddly enough, the man himself was not showcased in any of the pictures. Keith took many, many pictures. At some point, the raggedy man got distracted and went over to another table, talking to some other woman, forgetting about his ring. Katie would go home with it that night.

To be honest, I was glad that the raggedy man was gone. His departure, as small as it was, caused further celebration, probably because it alleviated a strange feeling that I was starting to have, so I ordered one last scotch.

Sometime in the middle of my having that scotch and of Ursula and Katie finishing whatever drinks they had, Keith realized that it was getting pretty late, that we had better leave - and soon. We paid our bills, piled back into Keith's HHR, and then he drove us back to his house. There, we sat, for a moment, in his living room, where he started talking to us about Mexico again.

"So, we're agreed that you'll come to Mexico to visit us then?"

He was talking to both Katie and I. Katie agreed enthusiastically, and I think that I might have nodded my head a little.

"It'll be a blast. You'll really love coming to Mexico. The culture! The weather! The people! The things to see and do! You'll *love* it! It is such a different world. Really. It's like you don't really know what's out there, what life is really like, until you get out of this country. You've got to get out of this country."

I was able, during Keith's lecture on the benefits of international travel, to regain some more of my composure, to appear presentable. I straightened my shirt, sat up straight, and brought focus to the forefront of my mind.

Maintain focus.

"You can come in March, it won't be too hot yet, but it'll be way better than being in Ohio. Trust me. Katie, you'll be on Spring Break, and Peter, I'm sure you can figure something out."

I nodded.

Katie looked awfully tired. She was still incredibly giddy, still pleased with her birthday celebration, unconsciously turning the ring in her hand over and over. But, I could tell that it would be time for her to go home soon; she would need lots of water, food, and sleep.

Unfortunately, Katie was in no condition to drive her car home. I think that Keith realized this too because he appeared to be a bit nervous as she got up to go. Sensing this, I stood up and said that I would drive her home.

"Peter, are you sure that you're okay to drive?"

Keith asked this with his forehead

tilted toward me, a sure sign that he was skeptical.

I decided to assure him.

"Yeah, I'm fine. I didn't have that much to drink. It's a short drive. She's not far from my house. Why not?"

I focused, hard, on maintaining my composure, and we all went outside. Katie gave me her keys, I unlocked the doors, and we got in. Keith and Ursula stood at his front door, smiling and waving goodnight to us.

ACCIDENTALLY

I had never been in a car like Katie's before. It was some sort of sports car, very flashy, very lightweight, rather low to the ground, and full of buttons and dials that I would never really understand. It was not as simple as my car. A wave of fear came over me as I sat there, wondering if I knew how to drive the damn thing.

In his chauffeuring us that night, Keith had made driving seem easy. In reality, the roads were a mess, as I soon found out. There was just enough snow and ice left on the streets to make turning slow and arduous and dangerous. Furthermore, I realized that, perhaps, I was not as ready to drive as I had previously thought.

Though I was no longer buzzed, I was fatigued, completely exhausted.

But there was no turning around now. I had to do it.

I tried to appear confident. I didn't want to frighten Katie. I had her best interests in mind in keeping all of this to myself. I would, calmly and slowly, take us, by way of back roads where no one else was driving, all the way back to her house, from which I would walk, through the snow, back home, less than a half dozen blocks away.

It was a simple plan.

The drive started off well enough. We used small, residential back roads and took it slow. Katie was still smiling and laughing and being delighted by the sarcastic and sharp commentary I made on various things. For most of the drive, I barely paid any attention to the things I was saying. I was just saying them, focusing, instead, on the road. Everything felt like ice; the whole street felt like ice, inches thick. The car could have been floating.

Halfway home, while rounding a corner in a residential neighborhood, after I misjudged the abilities of the car, we spun out and went into someone's yard. We were rather close to home, and so, while still not on a main road, we were in a more populated area at the time. I assured Katie that everything was fine and stepped out of the car. Watching her face, I realized that she believed me. She was completely unconcerned.

"This will just take a moment," I said, as though she could hear me through the glass.

Internally, I was freaking out.

I lit a cigarette because I knew that we were really stuck. This was bad. The two billon tons of white bullshit in this person's yard had us stuck here, stuck really good.

I tried to push the car, but it wouldn't budge under my strength alone. I thought about asking Katie to help, but she was blissfully unaware of how bad the situation really was.

While I was pondering the situation, looking under the front of the car at all of the snow that was trapping us, realizing that I couldn't get us out of this mess, trying to look busy and productive so as not to cause alarm, three teenagers, two boys and one girl, came out of the house. I straightened up, pulled the cigarette from my mouth, threw it away, and tried to decide whether this was a good or bad development. Were they going to bust me? Or were they going to save me?

"Are you okay?" the taller boy asked me.

"Yeah, just got stuck. Spun out a little. Misjudged it," I replied. I was trying to be terse, to not give myself away.

"Want us to help push you out?" the shorter boy asked.

"Yeah, just let me get in first so

that I can steer us right."

I was going to get away from them.

I got back in the car. Katie was, remarkably, still all smiles. This gave me a little hope.

I rolled down the window and told the boys to push. They did. The girl who was with them, still standing in the middle of the yard with her hands on her hips, just watched. I wondered if she was disapproving. Yet, at this point, it didn't matter. Things were looking as though they might work out for a change.

I steered the car as they pushed, and rather quickly, in what I recall as a surprising and elating moment, we were back on the road. I was sure that our tires had some, not much - but enough, traction to get the hell out of there.

Quickly - I got out of the car, handed the tallest boy twenty dollars, and told him to do something nice for himself, the other guy, and the girl. He thanked me, and they all went back into the house together, the two boys waving goodbye as they went.

I got back into the car, did my best to regain some composure (one last time), and drove Katie home.

Once home, she hugged me and said something, but being so tired at that time, drained from the bar, from the near catastrophe of being stuck out in the cold, from the waywardness of it all, I had no chance of remembering what it was that she said. I just recall, or imagine, that it was nice.

Then, being drained herself, she turned around and snuck back into her house so as not to awaken anyone.

I went back out into the night, walking now, alone in the snow. I jumped the gate to get out of her fenced-in community, which was actually very tough to do seeing as how the fence was so high. This made me vomit a couple of times, hard. Scotch isn't so good the second time around. Before continuing, though I still had some distance to travel before the night was over, I stopped to curse at the fence. Can't a guy just escape?

I trudged back home, chain-smoking as though it would keep me warm.

By the time that I finally reached home, I was exhausted and cold, with a

great deal of vomit spread over my
khakis. I cleaned up, quickly, only
barely, and went to bed, my self a
raggedy mess.

DISCOVERING

I woke up late the next day to a splitting headache. I laid around for the rest of the day, hoping to recover.

I thought about reading *Tell Them Who I Am* or *East of Eden*, but in the end, I figured that there wasn't any point in my doing so.

Finally, in the late afternoon, or perhaps the early evening, I felt better, made something to eat, and read for a while. It would have been a day without mention except for the phone call that came later that evening.

Katie called, thanking me for taking her home, talking about how wild the birthday celebration had been, and wondering why she had a ring on her finger. I told her that driving her home was no problem, added my own thoughts about how the celebration had been, and told her the story of the man who had given her the ring, not sparing her my own estimations of him - about which she laughed. I had thought the conversation was coming to a close, but she kept asking me questions, wanting to chat about small things, and laughing at my responses. Eventually, however, the conversation did wrap up. It took some time.

After that, I didn't hear from her or from Keith and Ursula for a while, which was fine since I had a mess of other matters to attend to in the meantime.

There was, for instance, the reality

that I wasn't getting much work. There would only be so much time before I became broke, which would be a real problem, especially when the college loan bills couldn't be paid. I dreaded that.

The other problems were less concrete, such as not knowing what more to do with my life. Substitute teaching, even in the short term, for the meantime, would obviously not be working out. What did I want? Should I, like Katie and Keith and Ursula, go for a Master's Degree? Based upon what I had studied as an undergraduate, I had very few options, or so I thought. I had a few applications, at home, on the table, piled up. But I hadn't bothered to read through them exhaustively. They simply sat there, gathering dust, making more of a mess.

The next day, Sunday, I laid around the house some more, took a few walks, read a couple dozen pages of a book, and thought out loud to myself. I considered, for a moment, going to church, but ultimately, that seemed pointless as well.

On Monday morning, no call came, and so, as to be expected, I was out of the house, wasting the morning away at the breakfast diner, and in the afternoon, I went to the library, which was also a temporary escape for me from time to time. In the late afternoon, I could, once again, go home.

On Tuesday, I finally received a call.

In a nearby city, Huron, I would be teaching gym classes, all day, at the middle school.

Gym classes are a mixture of the best and the worst of the substitute-teaching world. The lesson plans are never really all that complicated, though sometimes, they can be quite specific, almost incredibly so. Thus, teaching gym as a substitute makes for a less stressful day in terms of planning. The planning is not usually complicated or worrisome. On the other side of things, substitute teaching for gym classes can be very difficult in that the students take neither you nor the class very seriously.

On this particular day, the regular teacher, in her lesson plans, had me watching the kids while they shot basketballs in a free-for-all style. Her only note of any interest was "DON'T LET THEM GO ANYWHERE NEAR THE WOODPILE ON THE FAR SIDE OF THE GYM!"

This instruction was extremely clear, and it was equally hard to enforce. For whatever reason, the kids were drawn to that random woodpile at the far side of the gym; it was as though they could not help but gravitate towards it.

Near the end of the school day, I think it was sixth period, one class of kids simply couldn't seem to follow this instruction, though it was given to them multiple times. Finally, I raised my voice and yelled at them, "DON'T GO NEAR THAT WOODPILE!" A couple of minutes later, a heavyset teacher in a long black skirt and an Easter-blue blouse came into the gym on the far side. She just stood there, with her hands on her hips, staring, almost scowling, at me.

She obviously did not approve.

At first, I couldn't help but look at her quizzically, but after having her scowl at me for about a minute straight, I thought it best to just ignore her, to pretend that she wasn't there. In another minute or two, she was gone, but I already knew, by that time, that I wouldn't be coming back to Huron Middle School.

This would be only one more job, or multiple potential jobs rather, that I would not be getting.

The rest of the day went relatively smoothly.

I would be getting paid for this day, but still, I did not feel good, still anxious, because I knew, in the long term, that this wasn't going to work out.

My days were, in some sense, numbered.

I didn't expect to receive a phone call the next day, but by some grace, I did. I had a job at Huron High School, for the morning only, meaning that I would only receive half of a day's pay.

I was going to substitute for a chemistry teacher.

I came in early, studied the lesson plans intently, and read his note, which was written with heavy black ink and informed me that he might be back earlier than expected if all went well at his dentist appointment. I worked hard to really know the lesson, to memorize it, to be able to make the class sessions flow smoothly.

First, I would give a quiz. Then, I

had to, using a projector, teach the lesson, which I figured I could somewhat bumble through the first time and then embellish and polish for the next two class periods of the morning. After all of this was done, I was to play a review game with the students, present the homework, and give a little bit of guidance for it. This was a healthy-sized lesson plan, and I took to it with some gratitude, appreciating its substantial nature.

The first period class filtered in, with most of the students arriving on time. I took attendance and passed out the quiz. They only had ten minutes to complete it. Before the ten minutes were up, however, the regular, real teacher arrived back at the classroom.

Honestly, I was shocked to see him.

He nodded at me, took his seat at his desk, and began going through some of the papers there, putting them back into an order that suited him. In the midst of this, he looked up again, noticing that I was still there, just looking at him, and, with a wave of his hand, with a brushing gesture that one might use to shoo away muffleheads, he said, "You can go now. Don't worry - you'll receive your full pay for the day. Go ahead - you can go."

Full pay - a half day - that was incongruous, almost laughable.

I felt as though I had something that I wanted to tell him, but I didn't know what it was. I just sat there with something completely unformed on the tip of my tongue, wanting to talk to him, but I didn't know what it was that I wanted to say.

Realizing then that, maybe, I didn't have anything to say to him after all, I turned awkwardly, exited the classroom, walked down the hall, left the building, got into my car, and drove away, back to the breakfast diner to get some lukewarm decaf coffee…

Sitting in the breakfast diner, eating half-cooked scrambled eggs and some rather limp toast, knowing that I was being paid at that very moment to do nothing, I discovered, or was more convinced than ever, that this couldn't last, that it wouldn't hold up, that it was no good.

I thought about it so much that I developed a migraine. My head began throbbing with this splitting, threshing pain. Perhaps it was the coffee, or maybe it was all of the worrying, or it could have been that I was just so discontent… Whatever the case may have been, I was done with my whole situation.

With that feeling, in that same exact state of mind, I went to sleep that night.

ONE'S SELF

There was, of course, no phone call the next morning, but one came later in the afternoon – it was Keith.

"Peter, hey, listen, sorry I haven't called you sooner. Things have just been so busy, you know, with showing Ursula around and having her meet the family and working on her English and my German and you know – well – everything. But!… I'm sorry, do you have a minute?"

"Yeah, I'm not too busy today."

"Ok, good. Listen, I wanted to talk to you about this whole Mexico thing. I'm sorry that it went like that, that Katie got to talk to you about it before I did. I just really want you to come. I think it'll be good for you. Get out and see the world."

"Yeah, you'd said that."

"I know, I know. So what do you think?"

"Keith…"

I sighed while shaking my head.

"I don't know. I honestly don't know. It's going to be expensive."

"Peter, I'll get you the ticket, and you can pay me back whenever you're able."

This seemed like a nice lie.

"Keith, I don't want to do that."

"It's no problem really. Really, it isn't. I get points for all of the sky miles. So, in the long run, it really helps me out. Then you can just pay me back, either at once or piece by piece. It's real simple."

"How much are we talking about here?"

"The whole trip won't cost you more than two-thousand dollars."

I didn't even have two-thousand dollars.

"That's a lot of money."

"Peter! It'll be worth it! Trust me."

"I'll think about it."

"I'd really like it if you came. I think Katie would too. I think she really likes you."

"Keith…"

"Just think about it! Think about it for a while before you say yes or no. I'll give you some time. Okay?"

"Fine. I'll think about."

"Ok, great. Ok, look, I have to go, but I'll call you tomorrow. We'll all have to try to get together later this weekend. Maybe Saturday. I don't have much time left here. We'll have to get together again. Anyway. Ciao! Talk to you tomorrow!"

"Bye."

He hung up before I did, going off to do God only knows what with Ursula. I decided to take a drive, to take my mind off of things. Perhaps stop at the bank on the way and see how much money I had left…

IN THE MIDST OF A JOURNEY

My father lives in a nearby city, one that is, in my opinion, a bit nicer than Norwalk. It's a place called Vermilion. Sometimes, however, we meet in a place that is just a little closer to me, but not by much. On those occasions, we'll have dinner together at a place called Berardi's Family Kitchen, which is in Huron...

He called me Thursday afternoon and gave me a few orders, wanting me to go meet some man and pick up something for him and Donna. (Donna is my stepmother.) She and my father are always trying out new things with their house: new decorations, new furniture, new ways of setting things up. The house is always a little bit different whenever I get to see it.

So I went and did what he asked me to do, picking up things in Sandusky before heading over to Huron to meet him for dinner.

I was, to be honest, a little late. I had stopped to pick up a pack of smokes and ran into someone I had known in high school.

I think his name was Brandon.

I always dread running into someone I know from high school. They always want to know what you're doing now, but they aren't truly interested. Their asking doesn't seem to be out of concern for you or for the sake of really caring; they just want to know if you've surpassed them in life thus far or if they have been successful in comparison.

Luckily, Brandon didn't have too much to brag about. His mom had pulled that "you're eighteen, you're out of high school, and now you're out of the house" business on him. Ever since, he'd been living in the shady, project-like apartments behind the convenient store and working at the Ford Plant in Sandusky.

At least he was honest about how it was.

He had, of course, remembered who I was, though we weren't close, and he assumed some familiarity with me. But all he really knew of me was the crazy stunts that I had pulled while in high school. Other than that, he didn't know anything. So I played the part, as happens all too often. I told him that I was still up to the old madness, was getting away with it, and was, in general, doing well. That seemed to be more than enough for him, judging by the way that he just stood there and nodded his head.

I had thought, or assumed, that after that we would be done talking. But as I was about to leave the convenient store, having already bought my pack of Marlboro 27's, he asked me if I could give him a few dollars for a wine-flavored Black & Mild. I told him that I only used plastic, that I didn't have any cash on me.

"Oh," he said, and immediately, he looked down at the polished white tiles, at which point I walked out of the door, got into my car, and started driving to Huron.

I've never been in such a rush to see my father.

He was already seated at a table when I walked in. He was playing with his napkin-encased package of silverware, spinning it around on the table, looking down at it but obviously thinking about something else.

When I came over, he looked up and smiled. Then he rose from his seat and offered me a handshake. I shook his hand and we both sat down across from each other.

It was as though we were at a business meeting.

"How are you, Peter?"

"Good, and you?"

He asked me about what I had been up

to lately. I told him about hanging out with friends, about what I was reading, and about substitute teaching and how much effort it actually entailed. After some time, the waitress came over and took our order. Once she had gone, I turned the same question on him, inquiring about what he had been up to lately. He tersely spoke of being busy at work and about some of the great movies that he and Donna had seen in recent weeks. There was a period of silence after that, which I allowed and which was a mistake since it is usually after a period of silence that my father will start discussing something serious with me. It is always a mistake to give him a moment of silence to use as a pivot.

"So, have you thought about what you're going to do with your life yet?"

There is a good chance that another pause occurred here… Also a mistake, as it said more than I would have had I spoken.

"Things are going well."

"Peter. You can't substitute teach forever. What are you going to do with your life? You're living at home, with your mother. What are you going to do about your situation?"

"Something will come along."

Then, we both paused, the air full of things that either of us could say.

I thought (or rather - hoped) that we were done with the subject, but then it went on, with some of the things that were hanging in the air unsaid now being put to good use.

"If you do any graduate school, I expect you to pay for it."

The waitress brought us our food.

He had a Salmon dinner with asparagus. I had ordered the Cheese Burger with fries.

"Peter, I'm not made of money, you know."

"I know."

Suddenly, I wanted to be anywhere else, even the breakfast diner with the half-cooked eggs. This was a mistake.

"It'll be okay. I just need some time to figure it all out. Things aren't how they used to be."

"Figure what out? What is there to figure out? At some point, you have to decide what you're going to do with your life, what you can do, not just what you want to do, but what you can do."

"Right, right."

"You've got to make some money, Peter. You can't just keep doing nothing."

"I'm not doing nothing. I'm working. I'm thinking, planning. I've got an education. That's something."

"You've got debt."

"Right, right."

"You've got to do something, Peter! I'm telling you."

"I hear you."

Why do people insist on repeating themselves at great length - as though, by saying the words over and over and over again, something, the thing they want, will magically happen. You can't just speak into existence something that's not.

"You've got to, at some point, make a real decision in life."

At that, he probably figured he'd made enough of a point. More of a point than I'd like to admit.

He picked up his knife, and, with a bit of a heavy hand, stuck it into the fish, cutting it into fine, manageable pieces.

I just sat there and chewed on my burger. It was quite a while before we spoke again.

Norwalk, OH

I felt like dead meat.

A DECISION IS MADE

The next day, there was a great deal of snow. School was cancelled, so obviously, I didn't get a call. I was truly worried at this point.

I had no idea that dull, blunt anxiety could build this high. It was as though I was running from something - yet nothing was chasing me and I was going nowhere. Everything was uneasy and uncomfortable.

Thus, I frivolously wasted the morning away.

It was too cold outside to chain-smoke, so, lacking anything better to do, I went down into the basement, where, in large plastic bins (the hideous plain sort that people buy to stuff all of their other hideous junk into) all of my childhood and adolescent possessions now resided.

There were plastic toy dinosaurs, most of them rather generic, which had populated my fictional world of "Dino Land" when I was a kid. There were pictures of myself with friends, all of us on our bikes, wearing clothes that were just a little bit too big for us. There were stuffed animals and newspaper articles, including the front-page story on my high school graduation ceremony, where I had done the Heisman pose after walking across the stage, to the glee of the photographers waiting there. And, amidst all of the chaos, I found a laminated picture from the seventh grade. In the picture, smiling big, holding books we had made, were Katie and I and six of our fellow classmates.

I had completely forgotten that this had happened. I had remembered that we had made books, but I couldn't remember anything other than the mere fact of its occurring. The content, the people, what had happened while we were all making the books, and even the teacher were long past the reach of my memory.

So - there I stood. In the basement. In a dim room. With a box of old stuff. Doing nothing. Absolutely nothing. While, outside, all around, the snow piled up and suffocated out everything else.

I was going nowhere, and it was as though I had never been anywhere. I was always exactly right here, standing over a plastic bin full of junk from the past.

It was then that I made my decision.

TO GO

The next day, which was Saturday, I think, I woke up late, having dwelled on my decision for most of the night. I made some coffee - nasty, generic, store-brand coffee that came in a plastic cylinder. When it was ready, I went outside, where the snow was still piled up high, mercilessly and uselessly. I smoked three cigarettes in a row, went back inside, and snuck down to the basement.

For the next three hours, I went through all of my junk, taking it out of the plastic bins, examining it, appreciating it (or, at least, trying to), and separating it into two piles.

The first and smallest pile was comprised of those few things that I wanted to keep. The second pile, quite large, held the junk that I was going to sell to pawnshops or trade in at a local electronics store.

Out went the toy dinosaurs, out went the teddy bears given to me by high school sweethearts, out went the old comics and the baseball caps, out went dozens of Playstation games. Kept were a few old photos, a couple newspaper articles, and a belt with metal Cub Scout badges that I had forgotten I had ever earned.

I did archery? There's a badge for hiking?

Although I wasn't exactly thrilled to do it, I also collected up every videotape, cassette, DVD, and CD that I owned and put them into a box.

I worked for most of that day, sorting things out and then driving to local thrift stores to drop off donations, to a few dumpsters where I knew no one would see me illegally dumping trash, and to the electronics store where I could trade in my media for cash. The last of these errands was the one that took the most time. I had accumulated a lot of media junk.

When the trade-in was over, however, I was a little over five hundred dollars richer. I was on my way to Mexico.

It didn't take long to fall asleep that night as, for the first time in recent memory, I had hustled and worked hard.

Waking up the next day was peculiar, to say the least. I had cleansed myself of so many things, so many possessions. It had been a major undertaking (at least in my mind it had). There was a certain sense of pride in that, and in some ways, this pride was filling up the room, breathing life into the corners of my self that had felt vacant for a long, long time. Yet, the room also felt oddly empty. Cavernous. It was hollowed out, something of a formless void.

Waking up in this space, alongside the pride I felt, I sensed that something was wrong with me.

It was like waking up in depression.

Somehow, the space and my life, in my just-waking mind, had become conflated. Both were so full of void. So much was missing.

The space was messing with me. It became that which was most present in my life and had been present for a long, long time: nothingness. A great nothingness.

It was only an emptied room.

It was only an emptied room, but it made me want to cry, cry far more deeply than I had done in ages. And so, finally, I did.

And that too filled in some of the corners. And then, it too drifted away, as though it had been sucked into pre-dawn, pre-creation chaos.

I wondered - Just what the hell am I going to do with my life?

INTO THE WORLD

About a week later, after many anxious ponderings, only two substitute teaching job offers (in Norwalk itself, on Tuesday and Thursday), and a prolonged silence on the part of my friends, especially Keith, I received a call from John.

It had been a long time since I had last heard from John. For a number of years now, he and I had been butting heads.

To this day, I'm still not quite sure why John and I often find ourselves in the midst of a near-perpetual argument. He once said that this happens to us so often because we both have strong personalities, but I am close to attributing it to something larger, like two entirely different worldviews.

Though I was currently stuck in Norwalk, OH, John had been there more consistently, for an unbroken stretch of time, attending, for example, a very reasonable community college in the area. He was incredibly close with his family, working in his sister's restaurant on occasion, and had been at his job tending to vending machines since he was in high school.

In general, John was more at home in Norwalk, I think. He accepted it, as a tree accepts the ground on which it has been planted. I, on the other hand, though a native species, was not faring so well on this soil. I might as well have been an unhappy migrant from the East Coast.

Sometimes I look back and wonder if ever I started despising John for taking to this environment so wholeheartedly, as though he was missing nothing else in the world, as though this was where he was meant to be, for the little it had left to offer and the many things it would forever lack.

Nevertheless, despite whatever I may have resented about him, answering his call that day was a welcome return to something familiar.

"Yo, Pet-ah! You seen Adrian?"

He always used this greeting, taken from the Rocky movies and transformed to apply to whomever he was talking.

"No."

This was always my answer. What else

was one supposed to say to such a question?

It was just that stupid.

"What's up, John?"

In his normal voice now, he said, "Not much, man. So Jeffrey and I were getting kinda bored, and we thought it might be fun to, you know, go up to the Gore Orphanage and see if we couldn't find some ghosts."

"Are you serious?"

"Yeah, man. It could be kind of fun. Plus, what else are we going to do?"

Good question.

"Well, why not? I think I saw that once in a *Haunted Ohio* book. So, why not?"

"Alright, cool, man. Well, we'll pick you up around 7, alright?"

"Sounds good to me. Hey, uh, real quick, is Cory coming?"

I had been wondering how Cory was doing, but, sometimes, to ask was to hit a sore spot. I took the chance this time.

"I don't know, man. Haven't heard from him."

He paused, which was unusual.

"Last I heard though, he wasn't doing so well."

"Oh yeah?"

"Yeah, guess he missed some car payments or something. They took away his Blazer. His dad co-signed for him, so you know, his dad took a hit too. Couldn't have been happy. But, you know, that's all crazy, so…"

"No, I know. Well. Okay. So he won't be coming. That's alright. He probably needs to get things in order right now anyway. Doesn't need us to bother him."

"I guess so, man."

"Alright, well, I'll see you all around 7."

"Peace, Petey-Pete."

"Peace."

How strange. To not talk to someone in that long and then pick up again in our usual way, as though no time had passed, as though nothing had happened.

God, was this normal?

Later, at 7:00 p.m., just as he had said he would, John pulled up into my driveway. Jeffrey was in the front seat with a near-scowl on his face, as though he didn't really want to be where he was.

It wasn't a particularly cold night, but I came out with a scarf and a thick hunting hat anyway. I didn't want to be caught unaware. There was no telling what the three of us might get into on any given occasion.

As I opened the car door to get in, John hollered out, "Yo, Petey-Pete, what's up?"

"Nothing much," I said. "Let's get into some trouble."

I stole that line from *Requiem for a*

Dream, I think, but, despite his love of movie quotes, John didn't catch it. It was, to be honest, probably just a bit too obscure for him.

I looked over at Jeffrey. He just nodded, a slight acknowledgment of my existence. I supposed that was good enough.

"You ready for this, Pete? We about to find some ghosts!"

As we drove to Vermilion, John cracked jokes, told funny stories about his family and his co-workers, and, most consistently of all, did little, childish things to annoy Jeffrey. He would, with the tips of his fingers, reach under Jeffrey's chin and flick, quickly, either once or twice. Jeffrey would flinch and then, lamely, with one hand, try to shoo John away.

Next, John would, randomly, while driving, try to hug Jeffrey, which made Jeffrey irate, both because he felt that John should concentrate on driving and because Jeffrey doesn't like to be touched, especially by other men. John would also repeat the same annoying phrases and sounds to Jeffrey, over and over and over again. These noises could be any banal saying, popular catchphrase, or, more entertaining yet, strange, almost animal-like sound. Any sane person would go nuts from this constant barrage of passive abuse. Somehow, Jeffrey didn't go insane, though he may, at times, have come close.

And there I sat, in the back of the car, laughing at the absurdity of it all. It was amazing that we all put up with one another, I thought, but somehow, maybe, that's just what people in Northern Ohio are born to do.

Eventually, we arrived at the spot, on the edge of a sprawling woods, somewhere just south of Vermilion, Ohio.

Apparently, the area in which the orphanage was once located had become a state park because, on the side of the road, there were signs that said no one was allowed in the woods after dark. With the Gore Orphanage legend being as popular as it was, and with as many people as we had known to go in search of its remains at night, we didn't pay any mind to the signs. Didn't they know? This was a thing that people did - quite regularly, too. We were here, for better or worse, to see ghosts, and that's just what we would do, like the many who had come before us.

We took a couple of sodas out of John's car, thinking that it might be a bit of a trek, and then we began our journey. Not more than five minutes into our hike, I realized that I was ready to pee and have a smoke – one of the benefits of being in the woods at night. I told John and Jeffrey to go ahead a ways and that I would catch up with them in just a few moments. As they moved a little farther on, I turned around, found a nice tree, lit a cigarette, and relieved myself as a hard, cold breeze hit me and then flew through the woods.

I was staring up through the trees at the moon, which was shining just above a tall hill, when suddenly, on the hill, headlights rose up through the darkness of the night, slicing it open, and in its wake there followed alternate flashes of red and blue caressing the sky.

I cursed and threw my cigarette as far out into the snow as I could, not knowing whether or not it was legal to have a smoke in a state park. I called out to John and Jeffrey: "Guys, we've got company. The police are coming."

I could hear, through the crunching of the snow, John and Jeffrey walking back to me. Now they too were looking up at the hill, which the police car was steadily descending as it closed in on our location.

"We gotta get out of here," I said.

John just shook his head and made a futile gesture toward the hill with his whole arm.

"Can't. My car's back there; we gotta go out and meet 'em."

Though I was dreading it, he was right. Running away out here wouldn't do us any good. We simply couldn't run from this.

By the time we reached the edge of the woods, the police were already there.

There were two officers and both of them were standing behind their opened doors as though this were a bank robbery or a hostage situation. One of them had a bullhorn.

"GET OUT OF THE WOODS!"

Jeffrey was the first one out. He had both of his hands up in the air, stretched as high as they would go.

He walked, somewhat slowly, up to John's car and put his hands on the hood. He was ready for someone to frisk him.

John and I simply sauntered out of the woods, as though the police had requested an audience with us and we were now dignifying them by granting them this meeting.

The officer with the bullhorn was still using it, despite the facts that we were now in plain sight, clearly unarmed, and definitely not dangerous.

Who gives these idiots toys?

"COME HERE, SLOWLY," he said, and then he put the bullhorn away, somewhat hastily, realizing, perhaps, that it was superfluous.

The other officer looked at Jeffrey

and said, with a bit of contempt, "Stop doing that and get over here."

We walked over to the officers. They requested our IDs, which we gave them, and then they ordered us to sit and wait in John's car.

They must have been checking to see if we had criminal records, outstanding warrants, or some such thing because we were in the car for a long time.

Jeffrey was freaking out. He kept saying, periodically but repeatedly, as though it was a mantra or a prayer drained of confession or petition, "This always happens when I'm with you guys!"

John kept trying to make Jeffrey and I laugh. He said humorous things and attempted to make light of the whole situation. Typical.

To John, it was all one big joke. This time, however, no one was laughing. There simply isn't anything funny about getting stopped by the police, especially when one gets stopped for something stupid. Northern Ohio is no place for clowns.

At one point, one of the officers came over to the car and tapped, lightly with his knuckles, on John's window. John rolled down his window, and the officer, while sweeping the car with his flashlight, asked if we had any alcohol or drugs in the vehicle with us. John replied, "We got root beer!" He then held up a can of soda for the officer's benefit. The officer was not amused, but he was satisfied, knowing that someone this cheeky couldn't possibly have anything incriminating in his vehicle.

As for me, I grew quiet. Very, very quiet. And I waited for the time to pass.

HOWEVER

The next three days were filled with self-loathing, especially as how, on Monday and Tuesday, I received no calls for substitute teaching.

John, Jeffrey, and I had been given tickets for trespassing in the park after dark. The tickets themselves only cost us twenty dollars apiece; however, the court costs, whatever those referred to, added up to eighty dollars for each one of us.

Thus, I basically lost a hundred dollars, with no jobs forthcoming and with Mexico seeming farther and farther away.

Something had to change.

On the third and final day of loathing, while hiding away at the breakfast diner, I was reading the newspaper, thinking over and above the text and, instead, about the sorry state that I was in with everything, when, suddenly, a name caught my eye. It was the name of someone I had known.

I remembered Josh Westlake from the fifth grade. That year, my father had chaperoned a school field trip to the children's science museum in Columbus, Ohio. It would have been a smooth and easy trip if it were not for Josh Westlake. Josh was, especially at that early age, hyperactive, gregarious, and – most importantly – hilarious. My father had chased him around the museum that day. Josh kept breaking away from the group, disappearing entirely, and then reappearing to taunt my father in a fun-natured sort of way. The whole fiasco eventually evolved into a friendly rivalry, one which extended through the rest of that summer. Josh would stop by our house on his bike and, while enjoying light refreshments on our porch, joke around with my father in funny yet decent ways. The friendly rascality of it all impressed me, and for some time, Josh and I were friends, though, to be honest, most of the friendship was seated in his performing and my applauding. Eventually, and maybe inevitably, in the early stages of high school, as happens so frequently and fluidly when one is young, we drifted apart. It had never even occurred to me that we had drifted apart until I saw his name in the newspaper that day. It had all been so natural, for so much time to pass, for so many things to change. It was eerily natural.

He had died.

Although it probably would have been a just and decent, if minor, tribute to Josh had I exercised the integrity to read the whole article, I couldn't bring myself to do it. I simply skimmed over it, picking up enough information to know what had happened and to, in general, just feel plain awful.

On Route 6, in the early hours of the morning, he had crashed his car, killing himself. Thankfully, no one else was in the car with him. There was some speculation as to how and why he had crashed his car, but seeing as how none of the speculation was very flattering (as it rarely is in a small city), I stopped skimming the article and put the newspaper down. That was enough news for one day.

Thus, the three days of loathing ended with a brutal reality check, with a reminder of how things could go, that there existed a number of ways to not make it.

When your friends start dying, on top of the sympathy you feel for them and for their families, you realize that you're getting old, that things didn't go how you had once hoped they might go. You realize that, sometimes, and maybe more often than that, reality is brutal and hard and - yes - very, very real.

I never thought that, at age twenty-three, I'd be (basically) unemployed, sitting alone at a breakfast diner, eating dry pancakes, and reading about my (now) dead friend.

SOMETIMES

At the end of the week, on Friday, I got another call from John.

"Pete, this is John, don't hang up."

To be honest, I never had any intention of hanging up on John. The relationships between John, Jeffrey, and I, forming some sort of a triangle, were a little strained at the moment, especially since Jeffrey was angry with John and I because of the incident in Vermilion.

Somehow, in his mind, Jeffrey had fixed the blame for the whole thing onto John and I. He had found out, through a little research, that the legend surrounding the Gore Orphanage was just that, a legend. Several different stories from the area had collapsed together to form the giant myth of the Gore Orphanage and the ghosts that haunted it. In reality, only a mansion had burnt down, not an orphanage, and no one was inside at the time. Yes, there had once been an orphanage near the site, but it had closed down, not burnt up. The entire myth was a jumbled collage of the truth that formed a giant fiction.

Upon discovering this, Jeffrey could only think that John and I were stupid and look down upon us with not just a little scorn. Though, of course, he would never say this with words, only looks, and glancing ones at that.

It figures that, upon further examination, the entire backbone would fall out of the story and that, as is the case with so many ghosts in

Northern Ohio, it never really existed in the first place; there was only a lingering, haunting feeling, leaving much to be desired.

"What's up, John? Is Jeffrey still mad?"

"Oh yeah, he'll get over it. But listen, this is serious."

"What?"

"It's Cory. He's in trouble."

"Ok, come get me; we'll take care of it."

Usually, with John, it's a bad idea to agree to something before you know what it is – but in the case of a friend being in trouble, there's no point in asking for the details up front – you have to do what you have to do. It's generally as simple (and as consequently complicated) as that.

In less than a half hour's time, John was in my driveway, picking me up. He started explaining as he was driving us out of town, toward Route 2.

"It's Cory, man. He's in trouble."

"Yeah, what is it?"

"Well, okay, so I don't know the whole story exactly – but here's what I do know. So Cory's been really stressed out lately – you know – with money problems and stuff. And so, I guess he just freaked out and threatened to kill himself."

"What?"

"Yeah, he threatened to kill himself. Called up Laura and told her that he was seriously thinking about killing himself. So she talked him down, went over and got him, and took him to the hospital. Well, at the hospital, they transferred him over to another hospital, one in Toledo. Guess he needed real help."

"Ok..."

"Yeah, I don't know how all that really works, but I guess the fact of the matter is that he's up at this hospital in Toledo, in the psych ward, and I thought that we had better go and visit him. We are his friends after all; we should go see him."

"Definitely. But he's okay, right?"

"Yeah, as far as I know. I mean – I only learned about all this from his parents earlier today. They called me up and told me, because you know, we're his friends and whatnot."

"Toledo it is then."

We dropped the subject for a while, talking instead about the Vermilion experience, the steep court costs, and Jeffrey's reaction to it all. At that moment, it seemed that our small circle of friends was perpetually, in some unique-to-the-circumstances way, engulfed in crisis and disrepair.

Often, our question was: where had it gone wrong?

We drove near Toledo and ended up at a small hospital. The parking lot was surprisingly empty. John parked the car, and shuddering in the dense cold, we walked to the nearest entrance.

There was no one in the lobby. We

hadn't seen a single person outside or inside of this hospital yet. The dense emptiness made everything quiet and sterile. Instead of a receptionist, there was a red phone, the only object of any distinctive color in the lobby, placed, conspicuously, on the top of the unstaffed desk, facing outward.

I walked up to the phone and found, next to it, a note that instructed me to pick up the phone. So I did.

When I brought the phone to my ear, I found that it had already dialed out to someone, somewhere. Someone answered the call and asked me what I needed. I told her that my friend and I were there to visit another one of our friends who was committed to the psychiatric care unit. She instructed us to head down a few hallways, take a certain set of elevators, arrive at a specific floor, and be ready to sign-in upon our entry to the unit. It was all very clinical and hollow.

I thanked her for her help and then hung up the phone. I turned to John, who was giving me a look that expressed both his and my dismay at how creepy this hospital was becoming.

We followed the woman's instructions exactly, ending up at the psychiatric unit. She had guided us, from afar, with precision. We had to sign in, empty the content of our pockets, and submit ourselves to a brief search.

This, indeed, was serious.

After the brief search was over, one of the nurses went to retrieve Cory. We were to meet him in a nearby room that was specifically designated for visits.

John and I walked into the visitation room, which was cold and inflexible feeling, stocked as it was with hard and uncomfortable furniture. The way John examined the room by walking around it and craning his neck up and down and back again expressed his disapproval of it in a myriad of ways that I myself could never express with mere words. But I think it is fair for me to say that we both hated that room.

A few minutes later, Cory entered the room wearing a white beater and some ripped jeans. He greeted us warmly, as though our meeting in such a place was not abnormal, as though, somehow, this was the natural outcome of our years of friendship.

"What's up, guys?"

"Hey, man, how are you?"

He smiled. "Alright. Bet you never thought you'd see me here."

"You got that right."

After that, we proceeded to have a relatively normal conversation, despite our surroundings.

Cory was stressed. His finances had become difficult. He was frustrated, tired of fighting his circumstances. He'd had a moment of weakness and fatigue, and, though it wasn't done in the best possible way, he'd reached out to someone for help. So here he was to get help. I believed this, but the realization that we were in a psychiatric unit was nevertheless jarring. How can anyone ever be comfortable knowing that he or she is in such a place, even if he or she is only a visitor? It felt like insanity was a contagious pathogen.

Yet, the relative normalcy of our conversation was helpful in alleviating some of the tension, and, eventually, this relative normalcy overcame the permeating insanity of our immediate atmosphere, if only for a spell, and by the time that the visit was over, we were all joking and laughing as though we were somewhere else, like a bar, instead. In the end, we gave Cory a hug, said our goodbyes to him, and went to sign ourselves out of the unit.

As we left that desolate hospital, the spell of "normalcy" wore off, and once again, we were concerned about our friend.

What exactly did it mean that this had happened? What would this mean for the future? What exactly did this sign stand for?

There were no answers to these questions. The outlook was relatively dark. But then again, in non-life-threatening ways, things had been persistently dark lately, albeit only in a chronic and dull pain sort of way.

When things get like this in life, it seems that clichés come to mind all too easily, and during our ride home, in the moments of silence, cliché after cliché came to my mind, and I began paying more mind to them than they may actually have merited.

For example, they say that it gets darkest before the dawn. But, when people first started saying that, how did they ever determine what the "darkest" referred to in the analogue? Because, sometimes, it seems that deeper darkness just follows darkness, introducing you to ever-bleaker hues, surprising you because you didn't know, or believe, that it could get that deep - because no one ever told you that such a shade existed. Were there not entire worlds out there, floating somewhere, where no dawn ever arose, covered in permanent hues of snow and ice? And just what counted as darkness anyway? Did it only consist of the worst that could happen? I thought to myself that this is probably what most people meant by it. But that only led to other questions. Such as - what then is the worst? A life ended suddenly? A life wasted? A life technically ended but still living on anyway?

Finally, it became apparent that this line of thinking was incredibly unprofitable. I was having a strange argument with myself for no reason, trying to make sense of something by making sense of something else that made no sense. In the end, it was trivializing and demeaning to try to compare people's different definitions of darkness to one another. In the end, dark was just dark. Trying to figure out what the darkest was, in itself, was just an exercise in fumbling around in the dark.

Eventually, thinking continually in this loopy manner, I grew tired and fell asleep as John drove us home, through the snow and over the ice, back to Norwalk, Ohio.

THE GREAT ADVENTURE

On Saturday morning, I was busy crunching numbers, trying to figure out if the trip to Mexico was still really possible. If so, I needed to gather up my money, get it to Keith somehow, and let him make all of the arrangements, the flight, the bus ride to Xalapa, and the hotel room. I realized that if I was going to make this trip happen then I had to start substitute teaching more regularly. There was no other way, especially with the total amount of my bills and the added financial nuisance from the trouble in Vermilion. As I was figuring it all out, the phone rang. Suddenly, I had this feeling that I shouldn't answer it. But, what if it was a job offering, perhaps another day as a gym teacher?

"Hello, this is Peter."

"Peter, it's your dad."

Oh no. Not now. Not at this moment.

"Do you want to have dinner tonight?"

Despite the ominous coincidence of his calling while I was discovering the depths of my financial predicament, I told him that I would have dinner with him that night.

"Yeah, that sounds good."

"Great, I'll pick you up at around 6. I have a meeting before that, so if I'm running a little late, it's because the meeting has gone over."

"Okay, sounds good."

"See you later."

"See you later."

And we hung up.

After the phone call, trying to figure out my finances in order to get to Mexico wasn't as appealing. I sat down and stared at all of the work that I had been doing. These numbers were all little lies that I had been feeding to myself. There was no way that this was possible. I was not going to escape to Mexico. I simply wasn't going to get that many jobs in the next few weeks; I knew it.

I spent the rest of the day in the backyard, reading through Steinbeck's *East of Eden*. It was supposed to be his epic masterpiece. In some peculiar way, as the title hinted, it was meant to mimic the Bible, which itself was, technically, another great work of literature. Thus, for example, as with the Book of Genesis, one got to watch the development of a family line, quickly at first and then the work slowed down and one was able to focus in on one particular segment of the family line, a latter segment. Throughout, two sets of two brothers, first Charles and Adam and then Aron and Caleb, mirror the Cain and Abel story, with one brother always being innocent and the other always being dark and sinister-like. As I was reading, I appreciated what Steinbeck was trying to do, but it all felt too forced, as though the framework, rather than being a guiding hand, had become constrictive, and I thought it strangled some of Steinbeck's literary ability. Eventually, having covered a few hundred pages, I felt I had read enough for one day, especially as, in the case of the character "Kate" (previously known as Cathy), I was wondering if Steinbeck was a misogynist on some subconscious level. I left home, wandered around downtown, feeling restless, and only came back home much later, just before 6:00 p.m.

Shortly after I returned home, my father arrived to pick me up for dinner. He was dressed in his suit and tie, looking perfectly professional, as one might expect. I walked out to his Blazer and got in. He greeted me rather warmly.

"Good evening, Peter."

"Good evening. How are you?"

"Good. Did you get to work much this

week?"

He always got right to business, didn't he?

"Unfortunately, no. But I'm hoping that this next week works out well. It would really help if it did."

"Well, what did you do all week then?"

"It was a long week," I said lamely.

"Yeah?"

I was really going to have to answer his question, wasn't I?

"Phew. Well, we visited Cory in the psych ward yesterday."

"The psych ward?"

He had said this with some surprise and incredulity. When something shocks him, he expresses himself not so much with word choice or tone or inflection but with a quick craning of his neck forward and back, a rapid blink of his eyes, and a concluding stare that drifts off into space. This is how one knows that he has been shocked.

"Yeah, I was shocked too. It was...surreal. The hospital was vacant, almost deserted. It was like some disaster had struck."

"How was he?"

"He seemed normal, which helped at first, but the more I think about it, someone acting normally in a psych ward is out of place and strange in itself."

"Yeah, that is weird."

Then he changed the subject. He had probably heard enough.

"Where do you want to eat?"

We settled on a small, local Chinese restaurant, his favorite. The waitress seated us, took our drink orders, and left the table. As soon as she was gone, my father returned to business.

"So have you decided what you're going to do about your situation?"

I decided to just tell him.

"I was thinking about going to Mexico. It might be good for me to get out of the country, to see things, to get a contrast. Keith is going down there and-"

"Peter, Keith is in graduate school.

Of course he's going down there. That doesn't mean that you should go down there too."

"But why not? I might learn something."

"Peter, you're not in graduate school. You're not getting a degree in Spanish Education. You're substitute teaching in Ohio, and you're not even doing that very much."

No matter how old one has grown, there can come, in a conversation with one's parents, a moment where, for some almost-mysterious reason, your parents can, as no one else is able to do, touch upon the exact right pressure point, and if one is ready, aware, and in the right place to see it, there is then a consequent moment, seemingly outside of time, where one can preview and choose, like viewing paintings in a gallery, from a myriad of paths that one can take in the conversation, all of them generated by that precise, but gentle and correct, triggering of the pressure point. I had that moment.

I saw myself getting angry, indignant, stating my case in stronger terms, something like issuing an ultimatum. This is what I'm doing and that is final.

I saw myself becoming quiet - very, very quiet. I would murmur assent outside and disagree to myself inside. I agree, but I really don't agree at all.

And, last of all, I saw myself just admitting that he was right. The numbers, my father, the real business of it all, stated the facts plainly enough: this wasn't a good idea. If it were not for this then the pressure point wouldn't exist. It was better to just admit it and be rid of the pressure point altogether.

"You're right," I said, looking down at the tabletop as though I was hoping to draw some stability from it.

It was at this inopportune moment that the waitress decided to come over and take our order.

Couldn't she see that we were having a moment?

My father transitioned naturally into ordering his food - and so I did the same. When the waitress left again, I resumed my confession.

"You're right. It doesn't make much sense, does it?"

"No, it doesn't."

I never find it pleasant when someone answers a rhetorical question. But I proceeded anyway.

"I guess I need to figure something out."

"Peter, there's nothing here for you. Norwalk is becoming increasingly desperate. You need to start thinking about what you're going to do with your life. Substitute teaching won't work forever. You've got to get a big picture. Northern Ohio is just a small pond."

I felt that this was a little ironic in light of the entirety of our conversation, but there was no point in my saying such a thing as it would only make our conversation worse.

Despite my sense of irony, he had a good point and I had only just admitted it.

The conversation drifted on as usual, but for the first time in years, it was easier to get through. Though we hadn't settled anything per se, I felt mildly relieved. It was as though I had admitted to some addiction and committed myself to the road of recovery. There were no Twelve Steps for this sort of problem, but I felt like I had taken the first one.

Nothing was settled, but my father had successfully prodded me into truly figuring out the potential trajectory of my life. I was still lost, wandering in the wilderness, but at least now, I was trying to find some sort of a lead.

IT DOESN'T HAPPEN

When Monday came, I was grateful to get a call for a substitute teaching job. The call came early, around 5:00 a.m., and I was oddly excited. I flew through my morning routine, leaving time at the end to attend to such details as pressing my shirt well, leaving not a single wrinkle, and perfecting the knot in my tie. I had to leave earlier than usual as my job for the day, filling in for an art teacher, was in Sandusky.

I arrived at Sandusky High School ahead of schedule. This school, unlike some others in the area, was not unaccustomed to uniformed officers patrolling its hallways, bomb threats, and the occasional teacher scandal.

It was slightly drearier than nearby schools in that respect, but, with the sheer amount of hometown pride paraphernalia that littered the sides of the hallways, and an occasional trophy case showing up, this dreariness was slightly offset. I had the feeling that I was viewing a cave dwelling, dark, a little damp, smelling dank, that had, within it somewhere, tucked away in the deep, a homely fire roaring, keeping its inhabitants alive, perhaps it was located just around a corner.

I walked into the Main Office and waited for a teacher to stop chewing out one of the secretaries. After he was done and had stormed out of the office, I cautiously walked up to the counter and greeted the secretary. Without missing a beat, she smiled and asked what she could do for me. I told her that I was to substitute for the art teacher that day.

Still smiling, she said, "Ah, yes, you must be Peter then."

"Yes, that's me."

She gave me the key to the art room, told me that I should find the lesson plans on the teacher's desk, and gave me directions to the room. I thanked her and journeyed through the large, hollow hallways to the art room, which was located at the end of one wing.

Once inside, I made my way to the teacher's desk at the back of the room. The desktop was a mess of art projects, drawings and paintings and sketches. Searching through this mess, I began doubting that I would find any lesson plans, which was an awful realization since I knew nothing about art and was unable to make anything of value myself.

I was going to have to fake my way through this. For the next eight hours.

Feeling a little frantic, I began to go through the teacher's desk, something that I thought may have been a little out of bounds. Regardless, I plodded on, searching through his desk drawers, pulling out papers and skimming them to make sure that they were not emergency lesson plans. Many of the papers were just horrible, unfinished sketches, some were old attendance sheets, others were staff newsletters, and not a few were notes of the teacher's own making. In the third drawer that I searched, I found an interesting paper that made me stop and read it through in its entirety.

It was a copy of a letter that the teacher had obviously been forced to send to a concerned parent. In it, the teacher apologized, profusely, to the parent for waking up her child during class by tapping him on the head with a rolled up sheet of paper. The way that he described the incident, such as his using the word "tapping," made it sound as though the teacher didn't really feel that he needed to apologize for the incident. Yet, the utter amount of verbiage that he put into his apologizing – "I'm deeply sorry if I…" and "I completely regret…" – indicated that this was someone who was willing to grovel in order to keep his job, possibly one that he still loved, despite these unforeseen all-too-contemporary challenges.

I read through the letter twice, unable to believe that someone had actually had to apologize for something as harmless as tapping someone else on the head with a piece of paper.

This couldn't go on.

I never found the lesson plans that day, but the students, who were all in the middle of some project or another, knew, for the most part, what they were supposed to do.

A few chose to goof off, listening to music or playing on their phones, instead of working, but on this particular day, they were in the minority. I just let it happen. I knew that I could have challenged those students, but after having read through the teacher's apologetic letter, I decided that such an action wasn't worth it.

In the end, I was just some crappy substitute teacher, and I knew it - and I accepted it. It was better than being crucified on a cross made of cheap copier paper. It was better than groveling at the feet of some entitled parent. Plus, it was only art class.

The day went well enough. I hadn't said or done anything regrettable, and no one had caught me letting the students goof off. I babysat the students, turned in my key at the end of the day, and departed, hoping not to get called back to Sandusky.

& REALITY IS BRUTAL & HARD & VERY, VERY REAL

In some sick twist of fate, I was called back the very next day, back to Sandusky High School. This time I was supposed to teach English classes for sophomores. I chaffed at the thought of teaching high school sophomores; they were generally the worst of the bunch.

Thankfully, the teacher had left detailed lesson plans, making my life for the next eight hours easier than the entire day before. I had to read through the lesson plans twice. They were, in comparison with many of the other ones I had seen in the past, rather involved. Though, I should add, making comparisons between various substitute teaching lesson plans was, ultimately, a sad exercise as so many of them are unambitious, lacking any faith in the substitute teacher. Maybe rightly so.

The lesson plans dictated that, if I was able, I was to introduce John Steinbeck's *The Grapes of Wrath* to the students, stressing its importance in the world of American literature.

While doing this, I was to pass out the books to the students individually, recording which book was given to which student in the event that a number of them wouldn't be returned to the school. For this reason, each book had, in big strokes from a green permanent marker, a number written on the first page. After doing this, I was to put the sheet on which I had recorded the numbers into a secure drawer in the teacher's desk.

Next, I was to instruct the students to read the first four chapters of the book, which seemed like a lot but only amounted to about thirty pages. Still, for high school sophomores, this might have been ambitious.

I picked up the teacher's copy of the book and flipped through it, noting the length and contents of each of the four chapters. The first chapter was short and descriptive; it basically set the scene and the tone. The second chapter was a little lengthier; it introduced Tom Joad. If the students didn't appreciate this character then chances were that literature simply wasn't for them, though that was an un-teacherly thing to think. The third chapter was, again, short and descriptive. I had forgotten how often Steinbeck had punctuated this novel with little slideshow moments. Though tangential in nature, they added to the overarching tone and voice of the novel. In a way, they were actually quite brilliant, these little, picturesque chapters. The fourth chapter was by far the longest, and it was arguably the most important part of the students' reading for the day, but I wondered if they would actually have time to get to it. It was a long string of exchanges between old Tom Joad and Jim Casy. The latter was probably my favorite character of the novel, though Tom Joad was a close second. I was really hoping the students would get to this chapter, though I doubted the possibility.

While they were reading, the students were to answer questions on a worksheet that followed along with the reading. The worksheet was only two pages long, the front and back of one piece of paper. The questions were broken up according to chapter and some were more objective than others. For the shorter chapters, students were merely asked to report how the writing made them feel. The questions for the longer chapters asked about the characters and their exchanges. In total, it was not a tough assignment.

In the last ten to five minutes of class, I was to stop the students, if they were still reading, and go over the worksheet with them. After giving them the correct answers, I was to collect the worksheets. I could grade them while the next class was reading. It should, the teacher wrote, be a huge grade boost for many of the students. This was a sign.

The first two classes went smoothly. I began each class by waxing eloquently about the importance of *The Grapes of Wrath*, talking about how it shook the country, about how it forced people to think about the rights of migrant workers, how it humanized them. Steinbeck won the Pulitzer Prize for this work. It had been called "*The* Great American Novel," though the ghost of F. Scott Fitzgerald might have argued otherwise. The book had even caught the attention of Eleanor Roosevelt and provoked her into getting caught up in the struggle. Less flatteringly, Steinbeck was also demonized for this work, being called a leftist and a socialist, which actually weren't completely inaccurate descriptions. I talked a little bit about the Dust

Bowl and how devastating it was. I also provided a little bit of information on the slur "Okie" and how Ben Reddick had been credited as the originator of the term, whether or not that was true. In the second class, a student raised his hand at this point and asked, "His name was Ben Red-*dick*?" The class released some semi-suppressed laughter, but I kept moving on, explaining my expectations for the day and passing out the books and worksheets. So far, everything was going well.

Perhaps I was a better substitute teacher than I thought. Perhaps I was finally hitting my stride.

In the third class, I received a group of students who were particularly unruly. Upon entering the classroom and seeing a substitute teacher, many of them immediately pulled out their phones and their I-Pods and headphones. I tried to reason with them, but they only looked at me with loathing, their eyes staring me down as though I were a fraud. The ones who were left kept talking over my explanations. Many blatantly pushed aside the book and the worksheet, indicating that they simply weren't going to do it. I was dumbfounded by such outright insubordination. When it came time for the students to read, the trouble began to crescendo. One student, in the back, kept making loud noises, frightening screeches, like screaks from a dying animal. Some of the other students found this amusing, but a few were genuinely concerned. After nearly ten minutes of this nonsense, I finally called back to the student and asked him to stop.

"Whatever, man," he replied, "Like you're the teacher or something."

A minute later, he let out a screak so loud, so terrifying, that I was worried it would draw the high school's teachers into the classroom. I didn't need them to see this. Things had been going so well. I didn't need this now.

In a sterner tone, I asked the student to stop.

"Can you please stop now? You're going to disrupt the school. Please stop. And read your book."

"You can't tell me what to do."

"I'm the student teacher."

"You're the substitute teacher, dumbass, get it right."

That was the final straw. I stood up, pointed at the door, and said, "Leave. Now."

The student looked at me questioningly.

I pointed at him and then at the door.

"You. Leave. Now."

"Me, caveman. Me no go."

The students laughed.

Finally, I'd had enough. I didn't give a damn whether I'd be called back or not. This was a joke. Discipline was gone. It had left a long time ago. It was probably well on its way to California by now. I felt like whooping on this student's head with a rolled up sheet of paper myself. Maybe even with *The Grapes of Wrath*.

At least the act would have a touch of humor to it if I did. That would be enough to sustain me in prison, I thought.

But such a thing was, obviously, out of the question.

Instead, I did the only reasonable thing that was immediately at hand.

I yelled at the student, "LEAVE! NOW!"

The students were all shocked, as though I had just cursed them out in a flying array of colorful phrases. I thought that it was incredulous that this should be the thing that shocked them. Did nothing else that they had done over the course of the class period thus far shock them?

After I yelled at him, the disruptive

student became agitated, angry, uncontrollable. He got out of his desk, kicking it to the side violently. He strutted up through his row of desks, pump faked his chest at me as he passed, and went out of the door of the classroom in a huff, turning off the lights on us as he departed.

And we all just sat there, ignorantly, in the dark. The students were shocked. I was fuming.

After the commotion, a teacher came to the door, opened it, stood in the doorway with her hands on her hips, obviously angry now herself, and asked, sternly, if we were all right. I said that we were. Then she asked about what was going on. I told her that I had ordered a student to leave. Finally, she asked why we were all sitting in the dark. I thought that her final question was a good one, but I didn't answer it.

Figures that you'd come now, I thought.

Figures.

That was my last day of substitute teaching. Ever.

It was probably mutually beneficial that way.

AND

If I had thought that I understood loathing after the Vermilion incident, I was wrong. A new wave of self-hatred washed over me, with my own criticism and curses cutting at my vulnerable and exposed flesh like so many zebra muscles. I lurked around the city like a wounded animal, having finally failed at substitute teaching. It was not my calling in life. Yet, the situation was bigger than that as well. Not only was I not a teacher, not having the mettle for it, but in the wake of that failure, I questioned what I could be good at, knowing that the experience exposed my fortitude and temperament as being weak. You can't yell at students, no matter how bad they are. That's what contemporary conventional wisdom told us. You can't yell at students.

I was finished, and I knew it.

The breakfast diner began to lose all of its appeal that week. Not even the diner was a safe refuge anymore. I couldn't hide there any longer from myself, from my reality. I began taking long walks in nearby parks and nature preserves, which are not plentiful in Northern Ohio. The cold was unpleasant, yet there was something about it that was also oddly refreshing. It was like a touchstone for reality.

During those walks, I'd have long conversations with myself, trying to figure out what my next move would be. If not Mexico, then what? If not grad school, then what?

I didn't often come to many answers, but then again, when had I ever?

What was a person who was just becoming in the world supposed to do when he or she was in Northern Ohio, the rust belt, a place of declining opportunity, a place where hope felt hard won?

Ultimately, I settled on this as my question.

ONE SIMPLY MUST ACCEPT

At the end of the week, on Friday, I heard from Keith, he was back in Columbus already. Apparently, he had left Norwalk without saying goodbye. He would be heading to Mexico soon, and he wanted to know if I was going to come.

"Katie's already on board, Peter. She wants you to come."

"Keith..."

"Peter, listen. It really isn't all that expensive. It'll be a great adventure. Listen, it is so good to get out in the larger world. It gives you perspective. It helps you breathe. Whatever's bothering you, don't worry about it, just bring it to

Mexico with you, and I bet you that it looks different when you do."

"What if it looks worse?"

"It won't look worse."

"You can't possibly know that."

"No, I do, I do. Look, I've done this before, and I can tell you that, once you get some perspective, things are never really as bad as they seem. Sure, life looks pretty damn bad when you're just sitting in your hometown, wasting away, with bad employment, but once you step outside of that and are able to look around you, you realize how the world is bursting with opportunity. It's wonderful. You realize how much you're capable of and how many ways you can make the most of that capability."

"Keith, I think I basically lost my job this week. Things haven't been going all that well. I don't need to go to Mexico right now."

"Peter, Katie and I really want you to come. Ursula too. We'd all be really excited to see you. Especially Katie. Think about it. It's an opportunity. Don't you want to see if anything clicks with Katie?"

It had been a long time since I'd thought about Katie. My last real image of her was the one where she was sneaking into her parent's house on the night of her birthday. She was a nice girl, and on some level, I thought we clicked well.

But, at that particular moment, I wasn't feeling all that nice myself. It would never work. Katie, much like

Mexico, was just a well-intentioned but misplaced dream for me. There was no future for a relationship between her and I, though, as I knew, she was a wonderful girl. Perhaps, I thought, that was what made it impossible.

"I just don't think it'll work, Keith. She's getting her Master's Degree. I'm… I'm in Norwalk. That's it. I'm in Norwalk."

Keith spent the next half hour pleading, cajoling, enticing, and begging me to come to Mexico with them. He made promises, he tried to bait me, and he painted beautiful pictures of what might happen during our time down there. Yet, I knew, deeply, that each image was simply another little, necessary lie. It would keep me going, spin out the magic of it all for me, but in the end, I'd be right back in Norwalk, Ohio, following no plan in specific, drifting like dead wood in Lake Erie.

Keith would obviously go on to become a teacher somewhere. He'd be fluent in Spanish, well-educated, and living a comfortable middle-class lifestyle. Ursula, if she stayed with him, would be doing the same. Katie, training as she was for a lucrative career, had even more opportunities lying at her feet. She could pick up and move nearly anywhere so long as they had people who needed occupational therapy there. For her, Mexico was not a legendary undertaking; it was a well-deserved vacation and a rest stop on the fast track to a fulfilling, professional life. For me, it was a diversion, like so many diversions that already populated the Firelands area. It was about as useful as all of those videogames that I had sold off in my attempt to fundraise for the trip. I had merely traded in one false reality for another, potential false reality.

Eventually, Keith, frustrated and annoyed, gave up. He said a curt goodbye and that was the end of our conversation.

It was uncomfortable that our conversation ended so quickly. The let-down was asymmetrical to the build-up. So much had gone into Keith's trying to get me to go to Mexico, to chase this peculiar dream, but neither of us had a great deal to say in our collective realizing that it simply wasn't going to happen. Our scheming had been so bloated, but once I started to let the air out of it, it deflated quickly, with a short, sharp hiss, and then that was it. It was done. Over.

Keith could be pouty when he didn't get his way. I didn't expect to hear from him for a long time.

AS ONE IS IN THE PROCESS OF BECOMING

The next week was less cold than usual, yet the snow still remained on the ground, providing the same familiar hazard as always. I was still taking long walks in the parks and the nature preserves. This week, however, the walks were more bearable. The frozen beachfronts were beautiful to behold, a nice, though somewhat related, replacement for the hollow hallways at the high school. Somehow, this was better than working or sitting in the breakfast diner while pretending to be off at work.

After these walks, I found myself going to the library. There, I would sign up to use a computer, even though I had a far better one at home.

Something about the atmosphere helped to prod me along. It was quiet. The library was shaped like a giant medieval castle. A number of years ago, it was renovated, giving it an entirely new floor. Thus, on the outside, it looked like something from the dark ages, and inside, it spoke of more success than the rust belt had seen in decades.

How had this come about?

Online, I began searching for jobs. In college, I had, against the better judgment of my elders and mentors, studied religion. There was something about it that drew me in. Though – I should add – it wasn't the lists of rules or the fancy ceremonies that attracted me. It was the idea that, even though we had all been made so small in the past century, there was still something special about us, as well as over us.

Christianity itself, being the dominant Western religion, had been a large part of my studies.

To be honest, I wasn't very impressed by Christendom itself. The track record for Christendom was littered with Salem Witch Trials, Inquisitions, Heresy Trials, Post- and A- and Pre-millennial Ramblings (which I never understood), and questionable authority figures such as Father Charles Coughlin and Carry Nation.

The other side made more sense to me, the side that resembled a movement, one that only went from day to day, that had the small, personal view in its scope. Here resided Dorothy Day, Thomas Merton, and other socially-concerned saints. Through this side, hospitals and universities were brought about. People who were poor, people who had disabilities, people struggling in daily life - all of them were cared for in some way here. It wasn't always perfectly done, but then, as I knew well, not much was ever perfectly done.

I was always attracted to this side of Christianity. I thought Christ made a lot of sense when he preached Good News to the poor, the outcast, the downtrodden. I thought that Christ was right, and in being so right, maybe Christ was indeed God. At the very least, he stood a good chance of so being; Jesus was the closest thing to a god that I had ever seen.

I knew that not many of my friends would agree with me on these points, so on most days, I kept it to myself. I had, thus far, been a pretty terrible evangelist.

In my recent walks, however, thinking about my life as I had been, I realized that, though not a preacher perhaps, I at least connected with something larger, this idea that, somehow, even the least of us matter. I had been going about things all wrong. I had doubted this belief about people, in an extremely adolescent sort of way, especially about myself, and in recognizing that, I came to the conclusion that I too, though not making a popular move, belonged on this side of things.

At the library, I began researching jobs that might link up with my deeper beliefs about people. I found positions, all of which were low-paying, at homeless shelters, churches, food pantries, clothing banks, community centers, and group homes. A number of these postings were made for people with years of experience, which I obviously didn't have. Reading through these, the situation again felt hopeless. Yet, interspersed here and there, a foothold would appear, a position that appeared to be "entry-level." It was amazing that a person could just pick herself or himself up, move to a location, and begin employment in the social work profession. Though there wasn't much money in the work, I couldn't imagine better news than these jobs actually existing out in the world.

Unfortunately, the reality was that many of the jobs that appealed to me, working in a homeless shelter or a group home community, required me to move across the country, to Oregon or Georgia or Maryland. There was even a position in Vermont.

Which state was Vermont again, the one on the right or the one on the left? I always got the two confused.

The possibilities were almost dizzying. Yet, at some point, it dawned on me that I might be walking into another "Mexico." What were the chances that any of this would actually work out? Who was going to take an ex-religion major, someone who had failed in the world of substitute teaching, someone who was, for the time being, hiding out in his mother's house, waiting for something better to show up? The familiar waves of self-loathing began to roll in again.

When this happened, I left the library immediately. I got into my car and drove out to what I considered the best walking spot in the area, Sheldon's Marsh, a nature preserve.

Sheldon's Marsh is located near Route 6 in Huron. It seems to be tucked away, located around a turn in the road, flanked by trees. The parking lot doesn't give any real indication of what lies ahead. You simply park your car and begin heading down a long asphalt path. It starts off as a simple walk through the woods. Eventually though, the woods open up and marshland appears. In the summer, birds and squirrels run across the path, ducking into the woods or marsh shrubbery. In the winter, though not as lively, the scene is still one of beauty, only subdued. Underneath all of the snow and the ice, you can sense promise, a hint that something better will ultimately come along. It is as though all of the snow and all of the ice are there only to increase the surprise and joy and radiance of something new and green and fresh springing to life. Then, farther along, the marshes give way to the lake. Off to the side of the path, one can cut through the trees, entering private property, and stand on a relatively clean beach to glance out over the expanse, the lake, either rolling in perfect rhythm or frozen over, like the surface of another, distant world. The path ends at an abandoned NASA building and a stone breakwall. I don't think that people are supposed to climb up on the breakwall, but most people who visit Sheldon's Marsh do, myself being among them. On the breakwall, one gains a vista of the lake, a viewpoint from which to scan the horizon line. In the summer, one will see boats and jet skis, people flying by on their way to nowhere in particular. In the winter, one might as well be on the moon; there exists the feeling of being the only person left on earth.

In a few short months, everything will thaw out and life will come back, with full vibrancy. People will return from exile, and once again, they will populate this place. The birds and the squirrels will all run free, and one will never have guessed or known that such sheer amounts of snow and ice had ever existed here before. The thought will be far from their minds.

I felt like prophesying.

But as for myself, rather than

returning, I knew I was going to go out.

There was no longer anything here for me. Maybe there never was. But that never meant that there was not a Promised Land out there.

THE GROUND ON WHICH ONE STANDS

A few months later, I called John. His phone rang for quite a while, and I was just about to hang up when, contrary to my expectations, he answered.

"Yo, Pet-ah! You seen Adrian?"

It was nice to know that he was still comfortable and at home.

"No. What are you up to?"

"Oh, a little of this, a little of that, nothing too special. What's up with you, man? It's been a while."

"Yeah, it has."

I paused.

"Sorry about that. I – uh – this is weird to say, but I've been so wrapped up in what I've been doing that time just slipped away."

"Oh yeah?"

"Yeah, I've been looking for jobs."

"Well, that's good."

"Yeah, and I've found one. They offered me a position."

"Really?"

"Yeah, I think I'm going to move down to Georgia. Work in this group home community. It's called L'Arche. It sounds really nice. Like a fresh start."

He paused. I realized that it was a lot to drop on John. I should have given the information to him in pieces instead of handing over the whole load at once. But it was what it was.

He took a moment, cleared his throat, and finally found a response.

"That's really great, man."

There was another pause. I hadn't thought it would be like this.

"So when are you leaving?"

"Next week. I'm trying to leave and start there as soon as possible."

"Do we have time to get together?"

"Yeah...but let's not do anything too stupid this time around."

"I don't think Jeffrey will let us."

"You're talking to Jeff again?"

"Yeah, he always gets over it – eventually."

"That sounds about right."

"Well, look, let's get together this weekend then."

"If you say so. Just let me know where and when. I'll be there."

"Alright, I'll call you later this week and we'll set it up. Give you a good send-off."

"Right on."

There was yet another pause. I assumed that John was trying to think of something else to say. It was unlike him.

"And I'm really happy for you, man. This is good. Really good for you. I think that you needed this."

"Yeah, I did."

After that we said our goodbyes, a little flatly – probably because we both knew that this, for now, meant my moving on. It wasn't granted that we would stay in touch anymore, especially as I was being transplanted to somewhere new and because, as I assumed, John would most likely stay where his roots were, being absorbed with them as he usually was.

Looking back, I suppose that I called John first because, in contrast to me, he had always been at home in the rust belt, in Norwalk, OH. It was, to say the absolute least, a special environment, a place where things were fought for hard and where, despite this special effort, the laurels of glory didn't often appear.

Yet, for that reason alone, Northern Ohio deserves its credit. While it may only be "fly-over territory" for the people to the east and the west of it, this mid-Atlantic region hangs in the balance, trying to be a contender for something, even if that something never actually comes along.

It will, I believe, keep fighting on, and that, too, is what John will end up doing. He knows what he has to be in order to stay in this place.

As for me, there was, somewhere, whether in Georgia or not, something else in store. That much had been clear from the start. Neither I nor anyone else knew if I would actually do it though.

Packing my belongings, after having liquidated most of them for my (abandoned) trip to Mexico, was easy. There wasn't much to take along. Instead of a number of possessions, however, I had a few hard-earned lessons, or impressions at least, to take with me.

Norwalk, for as much as I complained (and still complain) against it, was and remains home.

And maybe for a reason. Maybe to knock down some of the entitlement that I had (and still have to some degree). Or maybe to teach me that there is a certain "way" to things, to the world, to inform me that nothing can be taken for granted, that, if I wasn't able or willing to take it up, opportunity would move elsewhere, among a different people.

More likely yet, maybe there was no real reason at all. Maybe "the reason" for this was just another ghost collapsing under the weight of its own myth. Maybe things were just the way that they were - and I should simply be grateful for that nonetheless - as bleak as that may initially sound.

The human mind can invent a reason around anything, and with something that I have both loved and hated as much as Norwalk, OH, I have wanted this place to have a certain kind of reason attached to it, the kind that imparts both a purpose and a blessing upon it.

I have wanted it to have a destiny.

Whatever I did wish, or still do wish, for Northern Ohio, it did, in the end, give me some sort of lead as to who I was becoming in the world, even if that wasn't perfect or pretty. It set me up, gave me all of the parts. It built me - for better or for worse. It commissioned me, and then it sent me out.

So maybe, rather than my blessing it, it blessed me, sometimes with curses.

It gave me a past, a starting point, but the responsibility of spinning that trajectory out, of following the winding line that I hoped went somewhere, was always my mine, never Norwalk's. That much I realized.

I was finally doing it, looking South, pushing past all of the snow and all of the ice. I was hoping to find something out there beyond all of that.

Saying goodbye to Norwalk proved to be harder than I had expected, especially when I could finally stand in a position that allowed me to appreciate it in its entirety, hardship and all.

But my bags were already packed, as meager as they were, and all that remained was for me to actually do it—

To go,

To head out,

To an unfamiliar land,

To be planted anew.

I didn't know whether to look to the sky or to the ground when I finally whispered the words, "Thank you."

So I did both.

ABOUT THE AUTHOR

Michael Hanck was born and raised somewhere in Ohio. He has worked as a Program Staff Person at a Daytime Homeless Shelter in the Pacific Northwest, a Live-In Assistant at L'Arche Harbor House, a Vicar at a Lutheran Church in New Hampshire, a Substitute Teacher in Columbus, OH, and was once a mighty fine Dishwasher at a Restaurant in Huron, OH. He lives in a new place every year or so, making it pointless to speculate about where he could now be living. Undoubtedly, wherever he is living, he will hike, read, write, brew beer, and eventually grow a beard.

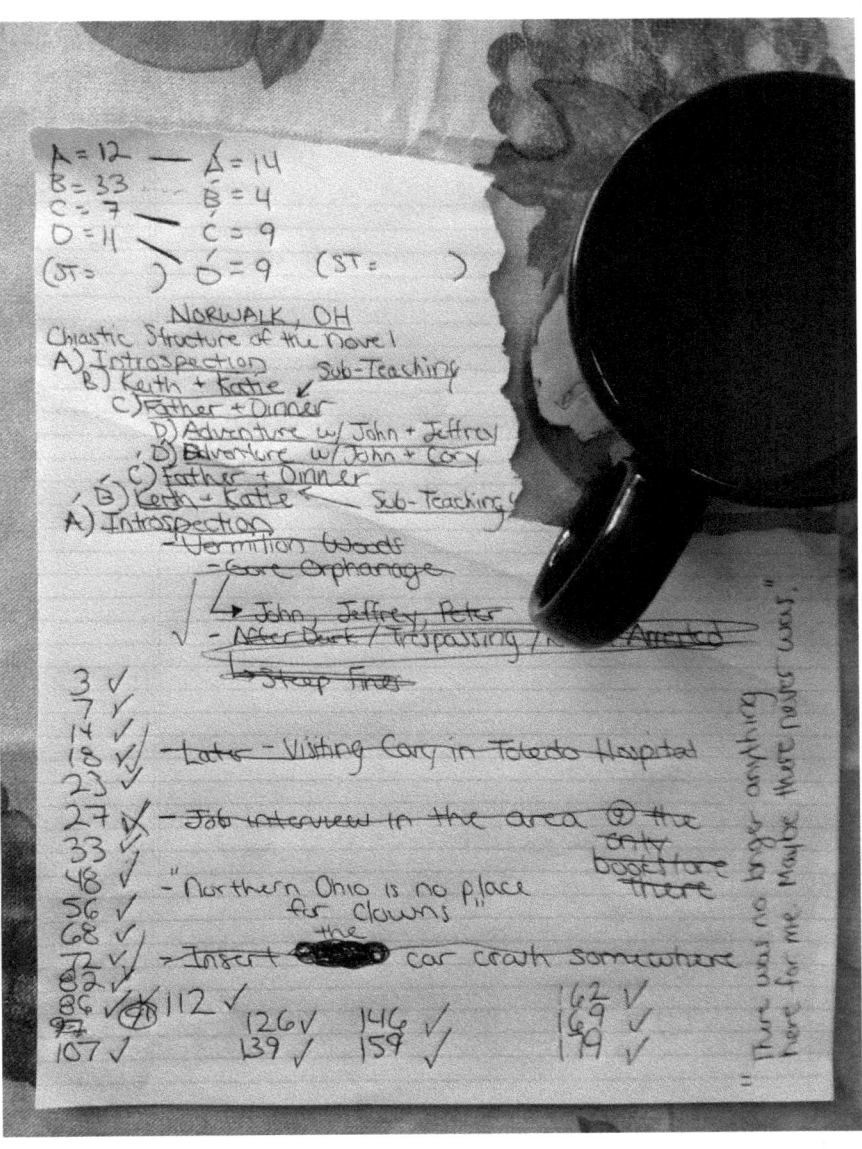

Lightning Source UK Ltd.
Milton Keynes UK
UKHW021848300920
370811UK00017B/189